GRAN

DOCTOR DEATH

Books by Jonathan Kellerman

DOCTOR
DEATH

Jonathan Kellerman

BCA

LONDON NEW YORK SYDNEY TORONTO

This edition published 2000
by BCA
by arrangement with Little, Brown and Company

CN 6684

Third reprint 2001

Printed in Great Britain by
Clays Ltd, St Ives plc

THIS ONE'S FOR
DR. JERRY DASH

1

I rony can be a rich dessert, so when the contents of the van were publicized, some people gorged. The ones who'd believed Eldon H. Mate to be the Angel of Death.

Those who'd considered him Mercy Personified grieved.

I viewed it through a different lens, had my own worries.

Mate was murdered in the very early hours of a sour-smelling, fog-laden Monday in September. No earthquakes or wars interceded by sundown, so the death merited a lead story on the evening news. Newspaper headlines in the *Times* and the *Daily News* followed on Tuesday. TV dropped the story within twenty-four hours, but recaps ran in the Wednesday papers. In total, four days of coverage, the maximum in short-attention-span L.A. unless the corpse is that of a princess or the killer can afford lawyers who yearn for Oscars.

No easy solve on this one; no breaks of any kind. Milo had been doing his job long enough not to expect otherwise.

He'd had an easy summer, catching a quartet of lovingly stupid homicides during July and August—one domestic violence taken to the horrible extreme and three brain-dead drunks shooting other inebriates in squalid Westside bars. Four murderers hanging around long enough to be caught. It kept his solve rate high, made it a bit—but not much—easier to be the only openly gay detective in LAPD.

"Knew I was due," he said. It was the Sunday after the murder when he phoned me at the house. Mate's corpse had been cold for six days and the press had moved on.

That suited Milo just fine. Like any artist, he craved solitude. He'd played his part by not giving the press anything to work with. Orders from the brass. One thing he and the brass could agree on: reporters were almost always the enemy.

What the papers *had* printed was squeezed out of clip-file biographies, the inevitable ethical debates, old photos, old quotes. Beyond the fact that Mate had been hooked up to his own killing machine, only the sketchiest details had been released:

Van parked on a remote section of Mulholland Drive, discovery by hikers just after dawn.

DR. DEATH MURDERED.

I knew more because Milo told me.

The call came in at eight P.M., just as Robin and I had finished dinner. I was out the door, holding on to the straining leash of Spike, our little French bulldog. Pooch and I both looking forward to a night walk up the glen. Spike loved the dark because pointing at scurrying sounds let him pretend he was a noble hunter. I enjoyed getting out because I worked with people all day and solitude was always welcome.

Robin answered the phone, caught me in time, ended up doing dog-duty as I returned to my study.

"Mate's yours?" I said, surprised because he hadn't told me sooner. Suddenly edgy because that added a whole new layer of complexity to my week.

"Who else merits such blessing?"

I laughed softly, feeling my shoulders humping, rings of tension around my neck. The moment I'd heard about Mate I'd worried. Deliberated for a long time, finally made a call that hadn't been returned. I'd dropped the issue because there'd been no good reason not to. It really *wasn't* any of my business. Now, with Milo involved, all that had changed.

I kept the worries to myself. His call had nothing to do with my problem. Coincidence—one of those nasty little overlaps. Or maybe there really are only a hundred people in the world.

His reason for getting in touch was simple: the dreaded W word: whodunit. A case with enough psychopathology to make me potentially useful.

Also, I was his friend, one of the few people left in whom he could confide.

The psychopathology part was fine with me. What bothered me was the friendship component. Things I knew but didn't tell him. *Couldn't* tell him.

2

I agreed to meet him at the crime scene the following Monday at 7:45 A.M. When he's at the West L.A. station, we usually travel together, but he was already scheduled for a 6:15 meeting downtown at Parker Center, so I drove myself.

"Sunrise prayer session?" I said. "Milking the cows with guys in suits?"

"Cleaning the stable while guys in suits rate my performance. Gonna have to find a clean tie."

"Is the topic Mate?"

"What else. They'll demand to know why I haven't accomplished squat, I'll nod a lot, say 'Yassuh, yassuh,' shuffle off."

Mate had been butchered fairly close to my home, and I set out at seven-thirty. The first leg of the trip was ten minutes north on Beverly Glen, the Seville fairly sailing because I was going against traffic, ignoring the angry faces of commuters incarcerated by the southbound crush.

Economic recovery and the customary graft had spurred unremitting roadworks in L.A., and hellish traffic was the result. This month it was the bottom of the glen: smug men in orange CalTrans vests installing new storm drains just in time for the next drought, the usual municipal division of labor: one guy working for every five standing around. Feeling like a pre-Bastille Royalist, I sped past the queue of Porsches and Jaguars forced to idle with clunkers and pickups. Democracy by oppression, everyone coerced into bumper-nudging intimacy.

At Mulholland, I turned left and drove four miles west, past seismically strained dream houses and empty lots that said optimism wasn't for everyone. The road coiled, scything through weeds, brush, saplings, other kindling, twisted upward sharply and changed to packed, ocher soil as the asphalt continued east and was renamed Encino Hills Drive.

Up here, at the top of the city, Mulholland had become a dirt road. I'd hiked here as a grad student, thrilling at the sight of antlered bucks, foxes, falcons, catching my breath at the furtive shifting of high grass that could be cougars. But that had been years ago, and the suddenness of the transformation from highway to impasse caught me by surprise. I hit the brakes hard, steered onto the rise, parked below the table of sallow dirt.

Milo was already there, his copper-colored unmarked pulled up in front of a warning sign posted by the county: seven miles of unfinished road followed, no vehicles permitted. A locked gate said that L.A. motorists couldn't be trusted.

He hitched his pants, loped forward, took my hand in both of his giant mitts.

"Alex."

"Big guy."

He had on a fuzzy-looking green tweed jacket, brown twill pants, white shirt with a twisted collar, string tie with a big, misshapen turquoise clasp. The tie looked like tourist junk. A new fashion statement; I knew he'd put it on to needle the brass at this morning's meeting.

"Going cowboy?"

"My Georgia O'Keeffe period."

"Natty."

He gave a low, rumbling laugh, pushed a lick of dry black hair off his brow, squinted off to the right. Focusing on a spot that told me exactly where the van had been found.

Not up the dirt road, where untrimmed live oaks would have provided cover. Right here, on the turnoff, out in the open.

I said, "No attempt to conceal."

He shrugged and jammed his hands in his pockets. He looked tired, washed-out, worn down by violence and small print.

Or maybe it was just the time of year. September can be a rotten month in L.A., throat-constrictingly hot or clammy cold, shadowed by a grimy marine layer that turns the city into a pile of soiled laundry. When September mornings start out dreary they ooze into sooty afternoons and sickly nights. Sometimes blue peeks through the clouds for a nanosecond. Sometimes the sky sweats and a leaky-roof drizzle glazes windshields. For the past few years resident experts have been blaming it on El Niño, but I don't recall it ever being any different.

September light is bad for the complexion. Milo's didn't need any further erosion. The gray morning light fed his pallor and deepened the pockmarks that peppered his cheeks and ran down his neck. White sideburns below still-thick black hair turned his temples into a zebra-striped stunt. He'd gone back to drinking moderately and his weight had stabilized—240 was my guess—much of it settling around his middle. His legs remained skinny stilts, comprising a good share of his seventy-five inches. His jowls, always monumental, had given way around the edges. We were about the same age—he was nine months older—so I supposed my jawline had surrendered a bit, too. I didn't spend much time looking in the mirror.

He walked to the kill-spot and I followed. Faint chevrons of tire tracks corrugated the yellow soil. Nearby lay a scrap of yellow cordon tape, dusty, utterly still. A week of dead air, nothing had moved.

"We took casts of the tracks," he said, flicking a hand at them. "Not that it matters. We knew where the van came from. Rental sticker. Avis, Tarzana branch. Brown Ford Econoline with a nice big cargo area. Mate rented it last Friday, got the weekend rate."

"Preparing for another mercy mission?" I said.

"That's what he uses vans for. But so far no beneficiary's come forth claiming Mate stood him up."

"I'm surprised the companies still rent to him."

"They probably don't. The paperwork was made out to someone else. Woman named Alice Zoghbie, president of the Socrates Club— right-to-die outfit headquartered in Glendale. She's out of the country, attending some sort of humanist convention in Amsterdam—left Saturday."

"She rented the van and split the next day?" I said.

"Apparently. Called her home, which also doubles as the Socrates office, got voice mail. Had Glendale PD drive by. No one home. Zoghbie's message says she's due back in a week. She's on my to-do list." He tapped the pocket where his notepad nestled.

"I wonder why Mate never bought a van," I said.

"From what I've seen so far, he was cheap. I tossed his apartment the day after the murder, not much in the way of creature comforts. His personal car's an old Chevy that has seen better days. Before he went automotive he used budget motels."

I nodded. "Bodies left on the bed for the cleaning crew to find next morning. Too many traumatized maids turned into bad publicity. I saw him on TV once, getting defensive about it. Saying Christ had been born in a barn full of goat dung, so setting doesn't matter. But it does, doesn't it?"

He looked at me. "You've been following Mate's career?"

"Didn't have to," I said, keeping my voice even. "He wasn't exactly media-shy. Any tracks of other cars nearby?"

He shook his head.

"So," I said, "you're wondering if the killer drove up with Mate."

"Or parked farther down the road than we checked. Or left no tracks—that happens plenty, you know how seldom forensic stuff actually helps. No one's reported seeing any other vehicles. Then again, no one noticed the damned *van*, and it sat here for hours."

"What about shoe prints?"

"Just the people who found the van."

"What's the time-of-death estimate?" I said.

"Early morning, one to four A.M." He shot his cuff and looked at his Timex. The watch crystal was scarred and filmed. "Mate was discovered just after sunrise—six-fifteen or so."

"The papers said the people who found him were hikers," I said. "Must've been early risers."

"Coupla yuppies walking with their dog, came up from the Valley for a constitutional before hitting the office. They were headed up the dirt road and noticed the van."

"Any other passersby?" I pointed down the road, toward Encino Hills Drive. "I used to come up here, remember a housing development being built. By now it's probably well-populated. That hour, you'd think a car or two would drive by."

"Yeah, it's populated," he said. "High-priced development. Guess the affluent get to sleep in."

"Some of the affluent got that way by working. What about a broker up early to catch the market, a surgeon ready to operate?"

"It's conceivable someone drove past and saw something, but if they did they're not admitting it. Our initial canvass produced zip by way of neighborly help. How many cars have you seen while we stood here?"

The road had been silent.

"I got here ten minutes before you," he said. "One truck. Period. A gardener. And even if someone did drive by, there'd be no reason to notice the van. No streetlights, so before sunrise it would've been pure black. And if someone did happen to spot it, no reason to give it a thought, let alone stop. There was county construction going on up here till a few months ago, some kind of drain line. CalTrans crews left trucks overnight all the time. Another parked vehicle wouldn't stand out."

"It stood out to the yuppies," I said.

"Stood out to their *dog*. One of those attentive retrievers. They were ready to walk right past the van but the dog kept nosing around, barking, wouldn't leave it alone. Finally, they had a look inside. So much for walking for health, huh? That kind of thing could put you off exercise for a long time."

"Bad?"

"Not what *I'd* want as an aerobic stimulant. Dr. Mate was trussed up to his own machine."

"The Humanitron," I said. Mate's label for his death apparatus. Silent passage for Happy Travelers.

Milo's smile was crooked, hard to read. "You hear about that thing, all the people he used it on, you expect it to be some high-tech gizmo. It's a piece of junk, Alex. Looks like a loser in a junior-high science fair. Mismatched screws, all wobbly. Like Mate cobbled it from spare parts."

"It worked," I said.

"Oh yeah. It worked fine. Fifty times. Which is a good place to start, right? Fifty families. Maybe someone didn't approve of Mate's brand of travel agency. Potentially, we're talking hundreds of suspects. Problem one is we've been having a hard time reaching them. Seems lots of Mate's chosen were from out-of-state—good luck locating the survivors. The department's lent me two brand-new Detective-I's to do phone work and other scut. So far people don't want to talk to them about old Eldon, and the few who do think the guy was a saint— 'Grandma's doctors watched her writhe in agony and wouldn't do a damn thing. Dr. Mate was the only one willing to help.' Alibi-talk or true belief? I'd need face-to-faces with all of them, maybe you there to psychoanalyze, and so far it's been telephonic. We're making our way through the list."

"Trussed to the machine," I said. "What makes you think homicide? Maybe it was voluntary. Mate decided it was his own time to skid off the mortal coil, and practiced what he preached."

"Wait, there's more. He was hooked up, all right—I.V. in each arm, one bottle full of the tranquilizer he uses—thiopental—the other with the potassium chloride for the heart attack. And his thumb was touching this little trip-wire doohickey that gets the flow going. Coroner said the potassium had kicked in for at least a few minutes, so Mate would've been dead from that, if he wasn't dead already. But he was. The gizmo was all for *show,* Alex. What *dispatched* him was no mercy killing: he got slammed on the head hard enough to crack his skull and cause a subdural hematoma, then someone cut him up, none too neatly. 'Ensanguination due to extensive genital mutilation.' "

"He was castrated?" I said.

"And more. Bled out. Coroner says the head wound was serious, nice columnar indentation, meaning a length of pipe or something like that. It would've caused big-time damage if Mate had lived—maybe even killed him. But it wasn't immediately fatal. The rear of the van was soaked with blood, and the spatter says arterial spurts, meaning Mate's heart was pumping away when the killer worked on him."

He rubbed his face. "He was vivisected, Alex."

"Lord," I said.

"Some other wounds, too. Deliberate cuts, eight of them, deep. Abdomen, groin and thighs. Squares, like the killer was playing around."

"Proud of himself," I said.

He pulled out his notepad but didn't write.

"Any other wounds?" I said.

"Just some superficial cuts the coroner says were probably accidental—the blade slipping. All that blood had to make it a slippery job. Weapon was very sharp and single-edged—scalpel or a straight razor, probably with scissors for backup."

"Anesthesia, scalpel, scissors," I said. "Surgery. The killer must have been drenched. No blood outside the van?"

"Not one speck. It looked like the ground had been swept. This guy took *extreme* care. We're talking wet work in a confined space in the dead of night. He had to use some kind of portable light. The front seat was full of blood, too, especially the passenger seat. I'm thinking this bad boy did his thing, got out of the van, reentered on the passenger side—easier than the driver's seat because no steering wheel to get in the way. That's where he cleaned most of the mess off. Then he got out again, stripped naked, wiped off the rest of the blood, bundled the soiled stuff up, probably in plastic bags. Maybe the same plastic he'd used to store a change of clean clothes. He got into his new duds, checked to cover any prints or tracks, swept around the van and was gone."

"Naked in full view of the road," I said. "That would be risky even in the dark, because he'd have to use a flashlight to check himself and the dirt. On top of operating in the van using light. *Someone* could've driven by, seen it shining through the van windows, gone to check, or reported it."

"The light in the van might not have been that big of a problem. There were sheets of thick cardboard cut to the right size for blocking the windows on the driver's seat. Also streaked with arterial blood, so they'd been used during the cutting. Cardboard's just the kind of homemade thing Mate would've used in lieu of curtains, so my bet is Dr. Death brought them himself. Thinking he was gonna be the trusser, not the trussee. Same for the mattress he was lying on. I think Mate came ready to play Angel of Death for the fifty-first time and someone said, Tag, you're it."

"The killer used the cardboard, then removed it from the windows," I said. "*Wanting* the body to be discovered. Display, just like the geometrical wounds—like leaving the van in full sight. Look what *I* did. Look who I *did* it to."

He stared down at the soil, grim, exhausted. I pictured the slaughter. Vicious blitz assault, then deliberate surgery on the side of an ink-black road. The killer silent, intent, constructing an impromptu operatory within the confines of the van's rear compartment. Picking his spot, knowing few cars drove by. Working quickly, efficiently, taking the time to do what he'd come to do—what he'd fantasized about.

Taking the time to insert two I.V. lines. Positioning Mate's finger on the trigger.

Swimming in blood, yet managing to escape without leaving behind a dot of scarlet. Sweeping the dirt . . . I'd never encountered anything more premeditated.

"What was the body position?"

"Lying on his back, head near the front seat."

"On the mattress he provided," I said. "Mate prepares the van, the killer uses it. Talk about a power trip. Co-optation."

He thought about that for a long time. "There's something that needs to be kept quiet: the killer left a note. Plain white paper, eight by eleven, tacked to Mate's chest. Nailed into the sternum, actually, with a stainless-steel brad. Computer-typed: *Happy Traveling, You Sick Bastard.*"

Vehicle noise caused us both to turn. A car appeared from the west, on the swell that led down Encino Hills. Big white Mercedes sedan. The middle-aged woman at the wheel kept to forty miles per while touching up her makeup, sped past without glancing at us.

"Happy Traveling," I said. "Mate's euphemism. The whole thing stinks of mockery, Milo. Which could also be why the killer coldcocked Mate before cutting him up. He set up a two-act play in order to parody Mate's technique. Sedate first, then kill. Piece of pipe instead of thiopental. Brutal travesty of Mate's ritual."

He blinked. The morning gloom dulled his leaf-green eyes, turned them into a pair of cocktail olives. "You're saying this guy is playing doctor? Or he *hates* doctors? Wants to make some sort of *philosophical* statement?"

"The note may have been left to get you to *think* he's taking on Mate philosophically. He might even be telling *himself* that's the reason he did it. But it ain't so. Sure, there are plenty of people who don't approve of what Mate did. I can even see some zealot taking a potshot at him, or trying to blow him up. But what you just described goes way beyond a difference of opinion. This guy enjoyed the *process*. Staging, playing around, enacting the *theater* of death. And at this level of brutality and calculation, it wouldn't surprise me if he's done it before."

"If he has, it's the first time he's gone public. I called VICAP, nothing in their files matches. The agent I spoke to said it had elements of both organized and disorganized serials, thank you very much."

"You said the amputation was clumsy," I said.

"That's the coroner's opinion."

"So maybe our boy's got some medical aspirations. Someone with a grudge, like a med-school reject, wanting to show the world how clever he is."

"Maybe," he said. "Then again, Mate *was* a legit doc and *he* was no master craftsman. Last year he removed a liver from one of his travelers, dropped it off at County Hospital. Packed with ice, in a picnic cooler. Not that anyone would've accepted it, given the source, but the liver was garbage. Mate took it out all wrong, hacked-up blood vessels, made a mess."

"Doctors who don't do surgery often forget the little they learned in med school," I said. "Mate spent most of his professional life as a bureaucrat, bouncing from public health department to public health department. When did this liver thing happen? Never heard about it."

"Last December. You never heard about it because it was never made public. 'Cause who'd want it to get out? Not Mate, because he looked like a clown, but not the D.A.'s office, either. They'd given up on prosecuting Mate, were sick of giving him free publicity. I found out because the coroner doing the post on Mate had seen the paperwork on the disposal of the liver, had heard people talking about it at the morgue."

"Maybe I wasn't giving the killer enough credit," I said. "Given the tight space, darkness, the time pressure, it couldn't have been easy. Perhaps those error wounds weren't the only time he slipped. If he nicked himself he could've left behind some of his own biochemistry."

"From your mouth to God's ears. The lab rats have been going over every square inch of that van, but so far the only blood they've been able to pull up is Mate's. O positive."

"The only common thing about him." I was thinking of the one time I'd seen Eldon Mate on TV. Because I had followed his career, had watched a press conference after a "voyage." The death doctor had left the stiffening corpse of a woman—almost all of them were women—in a motel near downtown, then showed up at the D.A.'s office to "inform the authorities." My take: to brag. The man had looked jubilant. That's when a reporter had brought up the use of budget lodgings. Mate had turned livid and spat back the line about Jesus.

Despite the public taunt, the D.A. had done nothing about the death, because five acquittals had shown that bringing Mate up on charges was a certain loser. Mate's triumphalism had grated. He'd gloated like a spoiled child.

A small, round, bald man in his sixties with the constipated face and the high, strident voice of a petty functionary, mocking the justice system that couldn't touch him, lashing out against those "enslaved to the hypocritic oath." Proclaiming his victory with rambling sentences armored with obscure words ("My partnership with my travelers has been an exemplar of mutual fructification"). Pausing only to purse slit lips that, when they weren't moving, seemed on the verge of spitting. Microphones shoved in his face made him smile. He had hot eyes, a tendency to screech. A hit-and-run patter had made me think *vaudeville*.

"Yeah, he was a piece of work, wasn't he?" said Milo. "I always thought when you peeled away all the medico-legal crap, he was just a homicidal nut with a medical degree. Now he's the victim of a psycho."

"And that made you think of me," I said.

"Well," he said, "who else? Also, there's the fact that one week later I'm no closer to anything. Any profound, behavioral-science insights would be welcome, Doctor."

"Just the mockery angle, so far," I said. "A killer going for glory, an ego out of control."

"Sounds like Mate himself."

"All the more reason to get rid of Mate. Think about it: if you were a frustrated loser who saw yourself as genius, wanted to play God publicly, what better than dispatching the Angel of Death? You're very likely right about it being a travel gone wrong. If the killer did make a date with Mate, maybe Mate logged it."

"No log in his apartment," Milo said. "No work records of any kind. I'm figuring Mate kept the paperwork with that lawyer of his, Roy Haiselden. Mouthy fellow, you'd think he'd be blabbing nonstop, but nada. He's gone, too."

Haiselden had been at the conference with Mate. Big man in his fifties, florid complexion, too-bushy auburn toupee. "Amsterdam, also?" I said. "Another humanist?"

"Don't know where yet, just that he doesn't answer calls. . . . Yeah, everyone's a humanist. Our *bad* boy probably thinks he's a humanist."

"No, I don't think so," I said. "I think he likes being bad."

Another car drove by. Gray Toyota Cressida. Another female driver, this one a teenage girl. Once again, no sideward glance.

"See what you mean," I said. "Perfect place for a nighttime killing. Also for a travel jaunt, so maybe Mate chose it. And after all the flack about tacky settings, perhaps he decided to go for scenic—final passage in a serene spot. If so, he made the killer's job easier. Or the killer picked the spot and Mate approved. A killer familiar with the area— maybe even someone living within walking distance—could explain the lack of tire tracks. It would also be a kick—murder so close to home and he gets away with it. Either way, the confluence between his goals and Mate's would've been fun."

"Yeah," Milo said, without enthusiasm. "Gonna have my D-I's canvass the locals, see if any psychos with records turn up." Another glance at his watch. "Alex, if the killer set up an appointment with

Mate by faking terminal illness, that implies theater on another level: acting skills good enough to convince Mate he was dying."

"Not necessarily," I said. "Mate had relaxed his standards. When he started out, he insisted on terminal illness But recently he'd been talking about a dignified death being anyone's right."

No formal diagnosis necessary. I kept my face blank.

Maybe not blank enough. Milo was staring at me. "Something the matter?"

"Beyond a tide of gore in the morning?"

"Oh," he said. "Sometimes I forget you're a civilian. Guess you don't wanna see the crime-scene photos."

"Do they add anything?"

"Not to me, but . . ."

"Sure."

He retrieved a manila packet from the unmarked. "These are copies—the originals are in the murder book."

Loose photos, full-color, too much color, the van's interior shot from every angle. Eldon Mate's body was pathetic and small in death. His round white face bore *the look*—dull, flat, the assault of stupid surprise. Every murdered face I'd seen wore it. The democracy of extinction.

The flashbulb had turned the blood splatter greenish around the edges. The arterial spurts were a bad abstract painting. All of Mate's smugness was gone. The Humanitron behind him. The photo reduced his machine to a few bowed slats of metal, sickeningly delicate, like a baby cobra. From the top frame dangled the pair of glass I.V. bottles, also blood-washed.

Just another obscenity, human flesh turned to trash. I never got used to it. Each time I encountered it, I craved faith in the immortality of the soul.

Included with the death photos were some shots of the brown Econoline, up close and from a distance. The rental sticker was conspicuous on the rear window. No attempt had been made to obscure the front plates. The van's front end so ordinary . . . the front.

"Interesting."

"What is?" said Milo.

"The van was backed in, not headed in the easy way." I handed him a picture. He studied it, said nothing.

"Turning around took some effort," I said. "Only reason I can think of is, it would've made escape easier. It probably wasn't the killer's decision. He knew the van wouldn't be leaving. Although I suppose he might have considered the possibility of being interrupted and having to take off quickly. . . . No, when they arrived, Mate was in charge. Or thought he was. In the driver's seat literally and psychologically. Maybe he sensed something was off."

"It didn't stop him from going through with it."

"Could be he put his reservations aside because he also enjoyed a bit of danger. Vans, motels, sneaking around at night say to me he got off on the whole cloak-and-dagger thing."

I handed him the rest of the photos and he slipped them in the packet.

"All that blood," I said. "Hard to imagine not a single print was left anywhere."

"Lots of smooth surfaces in the van. The coroner did find smears, like finger-painting whirls, says it might mean rubber gloves. We found an open box in the front. Mate was a dream victim, brought all the fixings for the final feast." He checked his watch again.

"If the killer had access to a surgical kit, he could've also brought sponges—nice and absorbent, perfect for cleanup. Any traces of sponge material in the van?"

He shook his head.

I said, "What else did you find, in terms of medical supplies?"

"Empty hypodermic syringe, the thiopental and the potassium chloride, alcohol swabs—that's a kicker, ain't it? You're about to kill someone, you bother to swab them with alcohol to prevent infection?"

"They do it up in San Quentin when they execute someone. Maybe it makes them feel like health-care professionals. The killer would've liked feeling legitimate. What about a bag to carry all that equipment?"

"No, nothing like that."

"No carrying case of any kind?"

"No."

"There had to be some kind of case," I said. "Even if the equipment was Mate's, he wouldn't have left it rolling around loose in the van. Also, Mate had lost his license but he still fancied himself a doctor, and doctors carry black bags. Even if he was too cheap to invest in leather, and used something like a paper sack, you'd expect to find it. Why would the killer leave the Humanitron and everything else behind and take the case?"

"Snuff the doctor, steal his bag?"

"Taking over the doctor's practice."

"*He* wants to be Dr. Death?"

"Makes sense, doesn't it? He's murdered Mate, can't exactly come out into the open and start soliciting terminally ill people. But he could have something in mind."

Milo rubbed his face furiously, as if scrubbing without water. "More wet work?"

"It's just theory," I said.

Milo gazed up at the dismal sky, slapped the packet of death photos against his leg again, chewed his cheek. "A sequel. Oh that would be peachy. Extremely *pleasant*. And this theory occurs to you because *maybe* there was a bag and *maybe* someone took it."

"If you don't think it has merit, disregard it."

"How the hell should *I* know if it has merit?" He stuffed the photos in his jacket pocket, yanked out his pad, opened it and stabbed at the paper with a chewed-down pencil. Then he slammed the pad shut. The cover was filled with scrawl. "The bag coulda been left behind and ended up in the morgue without being logged."

"Sure," I said. "Absolutely."

"Great," he said. "That would be great."

"Well, folks," I said, in a W. C. Fields voice, "in terms of theory, I think that's about it for today."

His laughter was sudden. I thought of a mastiff's warning bark. He fanned himself with the notepad. The air was cool, stale, still inert. He was sweating. "Forgive the peckishness. I need sleep." Yet another glance at the Timex.

"Expecting company?" I said.

"The yuppie hikers. Mr. Paul Ulrich and Ms. Tanya Stratton. Interviewed them the day of the murder, but they didn't give me much. Too upset—especially the girl. The boyfriend spent his time trying to calm her down. Given what she saw, can't blame her, but she seemed . . .

delicate. Like if I pressed too hard she'd disintegrate. I've been trying all week to arrange the reinterview. Phone tag, excuses. Finally reached them last night, figured I'd go to their house, but they said they'd rather meet up here, which I thought was gutsy. But maybe they're thinking some kind of self-therapy—whatchamacallit—working it *through*." He grinned. "See, it *does* rub off, all those years with you."

"A few more and you'll be ready to see patients."

"People tell *me* their troubles, they get locked up."

"When are they due to show up?"

"Fifteen minutes ago. Stopping by on their way to work—both have jobs in Century City." He kicked dust. "Maybe they chickened out. Even if they do show, I'm not sure what I'm hoping to get out of them. But got to be thorough, right? So what's your take on Mate? Do-gooder or serial killer?"

"Maybe both," I said. "He came across arrogant, with a low view of humanity, so it's hard to believe his altruism was pure. Nothing else in his life points to exceptional compassion. Just the opposite: instead of taking care of patients, he spent his medical career as a paper pusher. And he never amounted to much as a doctor until he started helping people die. If I had to bet on a primary motive, I'd say he craved attention. On the other hand, there's a reason the families you've talked to support him. He alleviated a lot of suffering. Most of the people who pulled the trigger of that machine were in torment."

"So you condone what he did even if his reasons for doing it were less than pure."

"I haven't decided how I feel about what he did," I said.

"Ah." He fiddled with the turquoise clasp.

There was plenty more I could've said and I felt low, evasive. Another burst of engine hum rescued me from self-examination. This time, the car approached from the east and Milo turned.

Dark-blue BMW sedan, 300 model, a few years old. Two people inside. The car stopped, the driver's window lowered and a man with a huge, spreading mustache looked out at us. Next to him sat a young woman, gazing straight ahead.

"The yuppies show up," said Milo. "Finally, someone respects the rule of law."

3

ilo waved the BMW up, the mustachioed man turned the wheel and parked behind the Seville. "Here okay, Detective?"

"Sure—anywhere," said Milo.

The man smiled uncomfortably. "Didn't want to mess something up."

"No problem, Mr. Ulrich. Thanks for coming."

Paul Ulrich turned off the engine and he and the woman got out. He was medium-size, late thirties to forty, solidly built, with a well-cured beach tan and a nubby, sunburned nose. His crew cut was dun-colored, soft-looking to the point of fuzziness, with lots of pinkish scalp glowing through. As if all his hair-growing energy had been focused on the mustache, an extravagance as wide as his face, parted into two flaring red-brown wings, stiff with wax, luxuriant as an old-time grenadier's. His sole burst of flamboyance, and it clashed with haberdashery that seemed chosen for inconspicuousness on Century Park East: charcoal suit, white button-down shirt, navy and silver rep tie, black wing-tips.

He held the woman's elbow as they made their way toward us. She was younger, late twenties, as tall as he, thin and narrow-shouldered, with a stiff, tentative walk that belied any hiking experience. Her skin tone said indoors, too. More than that: indoor pallor. Chalky-white edged with translucent blue, so pale she made Milo look ruddy. Her hair was dark brown, almost black, boy-short, wispy. She wore big, black-framed sunglasses, a mocha silk blazer over a long brown print dress, flat-soled, basket-weave sandals.

Milo said, "Ms. Stratton," and she took his hand reluctantly. Up close, I saw rouge on her cheeks, clear gloss on chapped lips. She turned to me.

"This is Dr. Delaware, Ms. Stratton. Our psychological consultant."

"Uh-huh," she said. Unimpressed.

"Doctor, these are our witnesses—Ms. Tanya Stratton and Mr. Paul Ulrich. Thanks again for showing up, folks. I really appreciate it."

"Sure, no prob," said Ulrich, glancing at his girlfriend. "I don't know what else we can tell you."

The shades blocked Stratton's eyes and her expression. Ulrich had started to smile, but he stopped midway. The mustache straightened.

He, trying to fake calm after what they'd been through. She, not bothering. The typical male-female mambo. I tried to imagine what it had been like, peering into that van.

She touched a sidepiece of her sunglasses. "Can we get this over quickly?"

"Sure, ma'am," Milo said. "The first time we talked, you didn't notice anything out of the ordinary, but sometimes people remember things afterward—"

"Unfortunately, we don't," said Tanya Stratton. Her voice was soft, nasal, inflected with that syllable-stretching California female twang. "We went over it last night because we were coming here to meet you. But there's nothing."

She hugged herself and looked to the right. Over at the spot. Ulrich put his arm around her. She didn't resist him, but she didn't give herself over to the embrace.

Ulrich said, "So far our names haven't been in the paper. We're going to be able to keep it that way, aren't we, Detective Sturgis?"

"Most likely," said Milo.

"Likely but not definitely?"

"I can't say for sure, sir. Frankly, with a case like this, you never know. And if we ever catch who did it, your testimony might be required. I certainly won't give your names out, if that's what you mean. As far as the department's concerned, the less we reveal the better."

Ulrich touched the slit of flesh between his mustaches. "Why's that?"

"Control of the data, sir."

"I see . . . sure, makes sense." He looked at Tanya Stratton again. She licked her lips, said, "At least you're honest about not being able to protect us. Have you learned anything about who did it?"

"Not yet, ma'am."

"Not that you'd tell us, right?"

Milo smiled.

Paul Ulrich said, "Fifteen minutes of fame. Andy Warhol coined that phrase and look what happened to him."

"What happened?" said Milo.

"Checked into a hospital for routine surgery, went out in a bag."

Stratton's black glasses flashed as she turned her head sharply.

"All I meant, honey, is celebrity stinks. The sooner we're through with this the better. Look at Princess Di—look at Dr. Mate, for that matter."

"We're not celebrities, Paul."

"And that's good, hon."

Milo said, "So you think Dr. Mate's notoriety had something to do with his death, Mr. Ulrich?"

"I don't know—I mean, I'm no expert. But wouldn't you say so? It does seem logical, given who he was. Not that *we* recognized him when we saw him—not in the condition he was in." He shook his head. "Whatever. You didn't even tell us who he was when you were questioning us last week. We found out by watching the news—"

Tanya Stratton's hand took hold of his biceps.

He said, "That's about it. We need to get to work."

"Speaking of which, do you always hike before work?" said Milo.

"We walk four, five times a week," said Stratton.

"Keeping healthy," said Ulrich.

She dropped her hand and turned away from him.

"We're both early risers," he said, as if pressed to explain. "We both have long workdays, so if we don't get our exercise in the morning, forget it." He flexed his fingers.

Milo pointed up the dirt road. "Come here often?"

"Not really," said Stratton. "It's just one of the places we go. In fact, we rarely come up here, except on Sundays. Because it's far and we need to drive back, shower off, change. Mostly we stick closer to home."

"Encino," said Milo.

"Right over the hill," said Ulrich. "That morning we were up early. I suggested Mulholland because it's so pretty." He edged closer to Stratton, put his hand back on her shoulder.

Milo said, "You were here, when—six, six-fifteen?"

"We usually start out by six," said Stratton. "I'd say we were here by six-twenty, maybe later by the time we parked. The sun was up already. You could see it over that peak." Pointing east, toward foothills beyond the gate.

Ulrich said, "We like to catch at least part of the sunrise. Once you get past there"—hooking a thumb at the gate—"it's like being in another world. Birds, deer, chipmunks. Duchess goes crazy 'cause she gets to run around without a leash. Tanya's had her for ten years and she still runs like a puppy. Great nose, thinks she's a drug dog."

"Too good," said Stratton, grimacing.

"If Duchess hadn't run to the van," said Milo, "would you have approached it?"

"What do you mean?" she said.

"Was there anything different about it? Was it conspicuous in any way?"

"No," she said. "Not really."

"Duchess must've sensed something off," said Ulrich. "Her instincts are terrific."

Stratton said, "She's always bringing me *presents*. Dead squirrels, birds. Now *this*. Every time I think about it I get sick to my stomach. I really need to go, have a pile of work to go through."

"What kind of work do you do?" said Milo.

"Executive secretary to a vice president at Unity Bank. Mr. Gerald Van Armstren."

Milo checked his notes. "And you're a financial planner, Mr. Ulrich?"

"Financial consultant. Mostly real-estate work."

Stratton turned abruptly and walked back to the BMW.

Ulrich called out "Honey?" but he didn't go after her. "Sorry, guys. She's been really traumatized, says she'll never get the image out of her head. I thought coming up here might actually help—not a good idea at all." He shook his head, gazed at Stratton. Her back was to him. "Really *bad* idea."

Milo strode over to the car. Tanya Stratton stood with her hand on the handle of the passenger door, facing west. He said something to her. She shook her head, turned away, revealing a tight white profile.

Ulrich rocked on his heels and exhaled. A strand of mustache hair that had eluded wax vibrated.

I said, "Have you two been together long?"

"A while. She's sensitive . . ."

Over by the car, Stratton's face was a white mask as Milo talked. The two of them looked like kabuki players.

"How long have you been into hiking?" I said.

"Years. I've always exercised. It took a while to get Tanya into it. She's not—let's just say this'll probably be the conclusion of that." He looked over at the BMW. "She's a great gal, just needs . . . special handling. Actually, there *was* one thing I remembered. Came to me last night, isn't that bizarre? Can I tell you or do I have to wait for him?"

"It's fine to tell me."

Ulrich smoothed his left mustache. "I didn't want to say this in front of Tanya. Not because it's anything significant, but she thinks anything we say will get us more deeply involved. But I don't see how this could. It was just another car. Parked on the side of the road. The south side. We passed it as we drove up. Not particularly close, maybe a quarter mile down that way." Indicating east. "Couldn't be relevant, right? Because by the time we arrived Mate had been dead for a while, right? So why would anyone stick around?"

"What kind of car?" I said.

"BMW. Like ours. That's why I noticed it. Darker than ours. Maybe black. Or dark gray."

"Same model?"

"Can't say, all I remember is the grille. No big deal, there've got to be lots of Beemers up here, right? I just thought I should mention it."

"You didn't happen to notice the license plate?"

He laughed. "Yeah, right. And the facial features of some psychotic killer drooling at the wheel. No, that's all I can tell you—a dark Beemer. The only reason I even remembered it was that when Detective Sturgis called last night, he asked us to search our minds for any other details, and I really gave it a go. I can't even swear it was that dark. Maybe it was medium-gray. Brown, whatever. Amazing I remembered it at all. After seeing what was inside that van, it's hard to think about anything else. Whoever did that to Mate must have really hated him."

I said, "Rough. Which window did you look through?"

"First the front windshield. Saw blood on the seats and I said, 'Oh shit.' Then Duchess ran around the back so we followed her. That's where we caught a full view."

Milo backed away and Stratton got in the car.

Ulrich said, "Better hustle. Nice to meet you, Dr. Delaware."

He jogged toward the blue car, saluted Milo as he entered. Starting up, he shifted into gear, hooked a U-turn and sped down the rise.

I told Milo about the dark BMW.

"Well, it's something," he said. Then he laughed coldly. "No, it's not. He's right. Why would the killer stick around for three, four hours?" He stashed the notepad back in his pocket. "Okay, one reinterview heard from."

"She's a tense one," I said.

"Blame her? Why? She set off some buzzers?"

"No. But I see what you meant about delicacy. What did she tell you when you spoke to her alone?"

"It was *Paul's* idea to come up here. *Paul's* idea to hike. *Paul's* a superjock, would live in a tree if he could. They probably weren't in the throes of love when they found Mate. Guess it didn't spice up their relationship."

"Murder as aphrodisiac."

"For some folks it is. . . . Now that I know about the second BMW I'm gonna have to log and do *some* kind of follow-up . . . hopefully a basic DMV will sync with some neighbor's vehicle and that'll be it." He rubbed his ear, as if dreading phone work. "First things first. Follow up with my junior D's to see how the family list is going. If you're so inclined, you could do some research on Mate."

"Any particular *theories* you want checked out?"

"Just the basic one: someone hated him bad enough to slaughter him. Not necessarily a news item. Maybe someone popping off about Mate in cyberspace."

"Our killer's a careful fellow. Why would he go public?"

"It's beyond long shot, but you never know. Last year we had a case, father who molested and murdered his five-year-old daughter. We suspected him, couldn't get a damn bit of evidence. Then a half year later, the asshole goes and brags about it to another pedophile in a chat room. Even then it was only a lucky accident that we heard about it. One of our vice guys was monitoring the kiddie-rapers, thought the details sounded familiar."

"You never told me about that one."

"I'm not out to introduce *pollution* into your life, Alex. Unless I need help."

"Sure," I said. "I'll do what I can."

He slapped a hand on my shoulder. "Thank you, sir. The suits are right miffed about a high-profile case popping up right now, just when the crime rate was allegedly dropping. Just when they thought they'd get some *good* publicity before funding time. So if you produce, I might even be able to get you some money fairly soon."

I panted like a dog. "Oh, Master, how wonderful."

"Hey," he said, "hasn't the department always treated you well?"

"Like royalty."

"Royalty . . . you and old Duchess . . . Maybe it's *her* I should be interviewing. Maybe it'll come to that."

4

I drove down Mulholland and eased into the traffic at Beverly Glen. The jazz station had gotten talky of late so the radio was tuned to KUSC. Something easy on the ears was playing. Debussy was my guess. Too pretty for this morning. I switched it off and used the time to think about the way Eldon Mate had died.

The phone call I'd made when I'd first heard about it.

No answer, and trying again was a much worse idea than it had been last week. But how long could I work with Milo without clearing things up?

As I tossed it back and forth, the ethical ramifications spiraled. Some of the answers were covered in the rule books, but others weren't. Real life always transcends the rule books.

I arrived home hyped by indecision.

The house was quiet, cooled by the surrounding pines, oak floors gleaming, white walls bleached metallic by eastern light. Robin had left toast and coffee out. No sign of her, no panting canine welcome. The morning paper remained folded on the kitchen counter.

She and Spike were out back in the studio. She had several big jobs backordered. With obligation on both our minds, we hadn't talked much since rising.

I filled a cup and drank. The silence was annoying. Once, the house had been smaller, darker, far less comfortable, considerably less practical. A psychopath had burned it down a few years ago and we'd rebuilt. Everyone agreed it was an improvement. Sometimes, when I was alone, there seemed to be too much space.

It's been a long time since I've pretended to be emotionally independent. When you love someone for a long time, when that love is cemented in routine as well as thrill, her very presence fills too much space to be ignored. I knew Robin would interrupt her work if I dropped in, but I was in no mood to be sociable, so instead of continuing out the back door, I reached for the kitchen phone and checked with my service. And the problem of the unanswered call solved itself.

"Morning, Dr. Delaware," said the operator. "Only one message, just a few minutes ago. A Mr. Richard Doss, here's the number."

An 805 exchange, not Doss's Santa Monica office. Ventura or Santa Barbara County. I punched it in and a woman answered, "RTD Properties."

"Dr. Delaware returning Mr. Doss's call."

"This is his phone-routing service, one moment."

Several clicks cricketed in my ear, followed by a rub of static and then a familiar voice. "Dr. Delaware. Long time."

Reedy tone, staccato delivery, that hint of sarcasm. Richard Doss always sounded as if he was mocking someone or something. I'd never decided if it was intentional or just a vocal quirk.

"Morning, Richard."

More static. Fade-out on his reply. Several seconds passed before he returned. "We may get cut off again, I'm out in the boonies, Carpinteria. Looking at some land. Avocado orchard that'll do just fine as a minimall if my cold-blooded capitalist claws get hold of it. If we lose each other again, don't phone me, I'll phone you. The usual number?"

Taking charge, as always. "Same one, Richard." Not *Mr. Doss*, because he'd always insisted I use his first name. One of the many rules he'd laid down. The illusion of informality, just a regular guy. From what I'd seen, Richard T. Doss never really let down his guard.

"I know why you called," he said. "And why you think I called back."

"Mate's death."

"Festive times. The sonofabitch finally got what he deserved."

I didn't reply.

He laughed. "Come on, Doctor, be a sport. I'm dealing with life's challenges with humor. Wouldn't a psychologist recommend that? Isn't humor a good coping skill?"

"Is Dr. Mate's death something you need to cope with?"

"Well . . ." He laughed again. "Even positive change is a challenge, right?"

"Right."

"You're thinking how vindictive I'm being—by the way, when it happened I was out of town. San Francisco. Looking over a hotel. Trailed by ten clinically depressed Tokyo bankers. They paid thirty million five years ago, are itching to unload for considerably less."

"Great," I said.

"It certainly is. Do you recall all that yellow-peril nonsense a while back: death rays from the Rising Sun, soon our kids will be eating sushi for school lunch? About as realistic as Godzilla. Everything cycles, the key to feeling smart is to live long enough." Another laugh. "Guess the *sonofabitch* won't feel smart anymore. So . . . that's my alibi."

"Do you feel you need an alibi?" The first thing I'd wondered when I'd heard about Mate.

Silence. Not a phone problem this time; I could hear him breathing. When he spoke again, his tone was subdued and tight.

"I wasn't being literal, Doctor. Though the police *have* tried to talk to me, probably have some kind of list they're running down. If they're proceeding sequentially, I'd be at the bottom or close to it. The sonofabitch murdered another two women after Joanne. Anyway, enough of that. *My* call wasn't about him, it's about Stacy."

"How's Stacy doing?"

"Essentially fine. If you're asking did the sonofabitch's death flash her back to her mother, I haven't noticed any untoward reactions. Not that we've talked about it. Joanne hasn't been a topic since Stacy stopped seeing you. And Mate's never been of interest to her, which is good. Dirt like that doesn't deserve her time. Essentially, we've all been fine. Eric's back at Stanford, finished up the year with terrific grades, working with an econ professor on his honors paper. I'm flying up to see him this weekend, may take Stacy with me, give her another look at the campus."

"She's decided on Stanford?"

"Not yet, that's why I want her to see it again. She's in good shape application-wise. Her grades really picked up after she saw you. This semester she's going the whole nine yards. Full load, A.P. courses, honors track. We're still trying to decide whether she should apply for early admission or play the field. Stanford and the Ivys are taking most of their students early. Her being a legacy won't hurt, but it's always competitive. That's why I'm calling. She still has problems with decision-making, and the early-admit deadlines are in November, so there's some time pressure. I assume you'll be able to find time for her this week."

"I can do that," I said. "But—"

"Payment will be the same, correct? Unless you've raised your fee."

"Payment's the same—"

"No surprise," he said. "With the HMOs closing in, you'd be hardpressed to raise. We've still got you on computer, just bill through the office."

I took a single deep breath. "Richard, I'd be happy to see Stacy, but before I do you need to know that the police have consulted me on Mate's murder."

"I see . . . Actually, I don't. Why would they do that?"

"I've consulted to the department in the past and the primary detective is someone I've worked with. He hasn't made a specific request, just wants open-ended psychological consultation."

"Because the sonofabitch was crazy?"

"Because the detective thinks I might be helpful—"

"Dr. Delaware, that's ambiguous to the point of meaninglessness."

"But true," I said, inhaling again. "I've said nothing about having seen your family, but there may be conflict. Because they *are* running down the list of Mate's—"

"Victims," he broke in. "Please don't give me that 'travelers' bullshit."

"The point I'm trying to make, Richard, is that the police *will* try to reach you. Before I go any further, I wanted to discuss it with you. I don't want you to feel there's a conflict of interest, so I called—"

"So you've found yourself in a conflictual situation and now you're trying to establish your position."

"It's not a matter of position. It's—"

"Your sincere attempt to do the right thing. Fine, I accept that. In my business we call it due diligence. What's your plan?"

"Now that you've called and asked me to see Stacy again, I'll bow off Mate."

"Why?"

"She's an ongoing patient, continuing as consultant is not an option."

"What reason will you give the police?"

"There'll be no need to explain, Richard. One thing, though: the police may learn about our relationship anyway. These things have a way of getting out."

"Well, that's fine," he said. "Don't keep any secrets on my account. In fact, when they do get hold of me, I'll inform them myself that Stacy's seen you. What's to hide? Caring father obtains help for suffering children? Even better, go ahead and tell them yourself."

He chuckled. "Guess it's fortunate that I do have an alibi—you know what, Doctor? Bring the police on. I'll be happy to tell them how I feel about the sonofabitch. Tell them there's nothing I'd like better than to dance on the sonofabitch's grave. And don't even think about giving up your consultant money, Dr. Delaware. Far be it from me to reduce your income in the HMO age. Keep right on working with the cops. In fact, I'd *prefer* that."

"Why?"

"Who knows, maybe you'll be able to dig around in the sonofabitch's life, uncover some dirt that tells the world what he really was."

"Richard—"

"I know. You'll be discreet about anything you find, discretion's your middle name and all that. But everything goes into the police file and the police have big mouths. So it'll come out . . . I like it, Dr. Delaware. By working for them you'll be doing double duty for *me*. Now, when can I bring Stacy by?"

I made an appointment for the next morning and hung up feeling as if I'd stood on the bow of a small boat during a typhoon.

Half a year had passed since I'd spoken to Richard Doss, but nothing had changed about the way we interacted. No reason for it to be any different. Richard hadn't changed, that had never been his goal.

One of the first things he'd let me know was that he despised Mate. When Mate's murder had flashed on the tube, my initial thought had been: *Richard went after him*.

After hearing the details of the murder, I felt better. The butchery didn't seem like Richard's style. Though how sure of that could I be? Richard hadn't disclosed any more about himself than he'd wanted to.

In control, always in control. One of those people who crowds every room he enters. Maybe that had been part of what led his wife to seek out Eldon Mate.

The referral had come from a family-court judge I'd worked with named Judy Manitow. The message her clerk left was brief: a neighbor had died, leaving behind a seventeen-year-old daughter who could use some counseling.

I called back, hesitant. I take very few therapy cases, stay away from long-termers, and this didn't sound like a quickie. But I'd worked well with Judy Manitow. She was smart, if authoritarian, seemed to care about kids. I phoned her chambers and she picked up herself.

"Can't promise you it'll be brief," she admitted. "Though Stacy's always impressed me as a solid kid, no obvious problems. At least until now."

"How did her mother die?"

"Horribly. Lingering illness—severe deterioration. She was only forty-three."

"What kind of illness?"

"She was never really diagnosed, Alex. The actual cause of death was suicide. Her name was Joanne Doss. Maybe you read about her? It happened three months ago. She was one of Dr. Mate's . . . I guess you couldn't call her a patient. Whatever he calls them."

"Travelers," I said. "No, I didn't read about it."

"It wasn't much of a story," she said. "Back of the Westside supplement. Now that they don't prosecute Mate, guess he doesn't get prime coverage. I knew Joanne for a long time. Since we had our first babies. We did Mommy and Me together, preschool, the works. Went through it twice, had kids the same years. My Allison and her Eric, then Becky and Stacy. Becky and Stacy used to hang out. Sweet kid, she always seemed . . . grounded. So maybe she won't need long-term therapy, just a few sessions of grief work. You used to do that, right? Working on the cancer wards at Western Pediatrics?"

"Years ago," I said. "What I did there was mostly the reverse. Trying to help parents who'd lost kids. But sure, I've worked with all kinds of bereavement."

"Good," she said. "I just felt it was my duty because I know the family and Stacy seems to be a little depressed—how *couldn't* she be? I know you'll like her. And I do think you'll find the family interesting."

"Interesting," I said. "Scariest word in the English language."

She laughed. "Like someone trying to fix you up with an ugly blind date. 'Is he cute?' 'Well, he's *interesting.*' That's not what I meant, Alex. The Dosses are smart, just about the brightest bunch I've ever met. *Individuals,* each of them—one thing I promise you, you won't be bored. Joanne earned two PhDs. First in English from Stanford, she'd already gotten an appointment as a lecturer at the U. when they moved to L.A. She switched gears suddenly, enrolled as a *student,* took science courses when she was pregnant with Eric. She ended up getting a doctorate in microbiology, was hired by the U. to do research. Before she got sick, she ran her own lab. Richard's a self-made millionaire. Stanford undergrad and MBA. He and Bob were in the same fraternity. He buys distressed properties, fixes them up, develops. Bob says he's amassed a fortune. Eric's one of those extreme geniuses, won awards in everything—academics, sports, you name it, a fireball. Stacy never seemed to have his confidence. More . . . internal. So it makes sense she'd be the one hit hardest by Joanne's death. Being a daughter, too. Mothers and daughters have something special."

She paused. "I've gone on a bit, haven't I? I guess it's because I really like the family. Also, to be honest, I've put myself in a spot. Because Richard was resistant to the idea of therapy. I had to work on him a bit to get him to agree. It was Bob who finally got through. He and Richard play tennis at the Cliffside; last week Richard mentioned to Bob that Stacy's grades had slipped, she seemed more tired than usual, did he have a recommendation for vitamins. Bob told him he was being a damn fool, Stacy didn't need vitamins, she needed counseling, he'd better get his own act in gear."

"Tough love," I said. "Must have been some tennis game."

"I'm sure it was testosterone at its finest. I love my guy, but he's not a master of subtlety. Anyway, it worked. Richard agreed. So, if you *could* see Stacy, it would help me not look like a complete idiot."

"Sure, Judy."

"Thank you, Alex. There'll certainly be no problem paying the bills. Richard's doing great financially."

"What about emotionally?"

"To tell the truth, he seems fine there, too. Not that he'd ever show it. He did have time to adjust, because Joanne was sick for over a year. . . . Alex, I've never seen such a negative transformation. She gave up her career, withdrew, stopped taking care of herself. Gained weight—I'm talking a tremendous amount, really huge, maybe seventy, a hundred pounds. She became this . . . inert lump. Stayed in bed, eating and sleeping, complaining of pain. Her skin broke out in rashes—it was a horror."

"And there was never any diagnosis?"

"None. Several doctors saw her, including Bob. He wasn't her internist—Bob likes to stay away from people he knows socially, but he worked up Joanne as a favor to Richard. Found nothing, referred her to an immunologist who did his thing and sent her to someone else. And so on and so on."

"Whose decision was it to go to Mate?"

"Definitely Joanne's—not Richard's, Joanne never told him, just disappeared one night and was found the next morning out in Lancaster. Maybe that's why Richard *hates* Mate so much. Being left out. He found out when the police called him. Tried to get in touch with Mate but Mate never returned his calls. Enough, I'm digressing."

"On the contrary," I said. "Anything you know could be helpful."

"That's all I know, Alex. A woman destroyed herself and now her kids are left behind. I can only imagine what poor Stacy's going through."

"Does she look depressed to you?"

"She's not the kind of kid to bleed all over, but I'd say yes. She *has* gained some weight. Nothing like Joanne, maybe ten pounds. But she's not a tall girl. I know how my girls watch themselves, at that age they all do. That and she seems quieter, preoccupied."

"Are she and Becky friends?"

"They used to be really close," she said. "But Becky doesn't know anything, you know kids. We're all very fond of Stacy, Alex. Please help her."

The morning after that conversation, a secretary from RTD Properties called and asked me to hold for Mr. Doss. Pop music played for several minutes and then Richard came on sounding alert, almost cheerful, not at all like a man whose wife had killed herself three months before. Then again, as Judy had said, he'd had time to prepare.

No hint of the resistance Judy had described. He sounded eager, as if readying himself for a new challenge.

Then he began laying out the rules.

No more of that "Mr. Doss," Doctor. Call me Richard.

Services to be billed monthly through my corporate office, here's the number.

Stacy can't afford to miss school, so late-afternoon appointments are essential.

I expect some definition of the process you foresee, specifically what kind of treatment is called for and how long it will take.

Once you've completed your preliminary findings, please submit them to me in writing and we'll take it from there.

"How old is Stacy?" I said.

"She turned seventeen last month."

"There's something you should know, then. Legally, she has no rights to confidentiality. But I can't work with a teen unless the parent agrees to respect confidentiality."

"Meaning I'm shut out of the process."

"Not necessarily . . ."

"Fine. When can I bring her in?"

"One more thing," I said. "I'll need to see you first."

"Why?"

"Before I see a patient, I take a complete history from the parent."

"I don't know about that. I'm extraordinarily busy, right in the middle of some complex deals. What would be the point, Doctor? We're focusing on a rather discrete topic: Stacy's grief. Not her infancy. I could see her development being relevant if it was a learning disability or some kind of immaturity, but any school problems she's experiencing have got to be a reaction to her mother's death. Don't get me wrong, I understand all about family therapy, but that's not what's called for here.

"I consulted a family therapist when my wife's illness intensified. Some quack referred by a doctor I no longer employ, because he felt someone should inquire about Stacy and Eric. I was reluctant, but I complied. The quack kept pressuring me to get the entire family involved, including Joanne. One of those New Agey types, miniature fountain in the waiting room, patronizing voice. I thought it was absolute nonsense. Judy Manitow claims you're quite good."

His tone implied Judy was well-meaning but far from infallible.

I said, "Whatever form treatment takes, Mr. Doss—"

"Richard."

"I'll need to see you first."

"Can't we do history-taking over the phone? Isn't that what we're doing right now? Look, if payment's the issue, just bill me for telephonic services. God knows my lawyers do."

"It's not that," I said. "I need to meet you face-to-face."

"Why?"

"It's the way I work, Richard."

"Well," he said. "That sounds rather dogmatic. The quack insisted on family therapy and you insist upon face-to-face."

"I've found it to be the best way."

"And if I don't agree?"

"Then I'm sorry, but I won't be able to see your daughter."

His chuckle was flat, percussive. I thought of a mechanical noise-maker. "You must be busy to afford to be that cavalier, Doctor. Congratulations."

Neither of us talked for several seconds and I wondered if I'd erred. The man had been through hell, why not be flexible? But something in his manner had gotten to me—the truth was, he'd pushed, so I'd pushed back. Amateur hour, Delaware. I should've known better.

I was about to back off when he said, "All right, I admire a man with spine. I'll see you once. But not this week, I'm out of town. . . . Let me check my calendar . . . hold on."

Click. On hold again. More pop music, belch-tone synthesizer syrup in waltz-time. "Tuesday at six is my only window this week, Doctor."

"Fine."

"Not *that* busy, eh? Give me your address."

I did.

"That's residential," he said.

"I work out of my house."

"Makes sense, keep the overhead down. Okay, see you Tuesday. In the meantime, you can begin with Stacy on Monday. She'll be available anytime after school—"

"I'll see her after we've spoken, Richard."

"What a *tough* sonofabitch you are, Doctor. Should've gone into *my* business. The money's a helluva lot better and you could still work out of your house."

5

An alibi.

Richard's call made me want to get out of the house. I filled a cup for Robin and carried it, along with mine, out through the house and into the garden. Passing the perennial bed Robin had laid down last winter, crossing the footbridge to the pond, the rock waterfall. Placing the coffee on a stone bench, I paused to toss pellets to the koi. The fish darted toward me before the food hit the water, coalescing in a frothy swirl at the rim. Iron skies bore down, dyeing the water charcoal, playing on metallic scales. The air was cool, odorless, just as stagnant as up at the murder site, but greenery and water burble blunted the sense of lifelessness.

Up in the hills, September haze can be romanticized as fog. Our property's not large, but it's secluded because of an unbuildable western border, and surrounded by old-growth pines and lemon gums that create the illusion of solitude. This morning the treetops were capped with gray.

I crouched, allowing one of the larger carp to nibble my fingers. Reminding myself, as I sometimes did, that life was transitory and I was lucky to be living amid beauty and relative quiet. My father destroyed himself with alcohol and my mother was heroic but habitually sad. No whining, the past isn't a straitjacket. But for people breast-fed on misery, it can be an awfully tight sweater.

No sounds from the studio, then the chip-chip of Robin's chisel. The building's a single-story miniature of the house, with high windows and an old, burnished pine door rescued by Robin from a downtown demolition. I pushed the door open, heard music playing softly—Ry Cooder on slide. Robin was at her workbench, hair tied up in a red silk scarf, wearing gray denim overalls over a black T-shirt. Hunched in a way that would cause her shoulders to ache by nightfall. She didn't hear me enter. Smooth, slender arms worked the chisel on a guitar-shaped piece of Alaskan spruce. Wood shavings curled at her feet, creating a cozy bed for Spike. His bulldog bulk had sunk into the scrap, and he snored away, flews flapping.

I watched for a while as Robin continued to tune the soundboard, tapping, chiseling, tapping again, running her fingers along the inner edges, pausing to reflect before resuming. Her wrists were child-size, seemed too fragile to manipulate steel, but she handled the tool as if it was a chopstick.

Biting her lower lip, then licking it, as her back humped more acutely. A stray bit of auburn curl sprang loose from the kerchief and she tucked it back impatiently. Oblivious to my presence though I stood ten, fifteen feet away. As with most creative people, time and space have no meaning for her when her mind's engaged.

I came closer, stopped at the far end of the bench. Mahogany eyes widened, she placed the chisel on the workbench and the ivory flash of those two oversize incisors appeared between full, soft lips. I smiled back and held out a cup, enjoying the contours of her face, heart-shaped, olive-tinted, decorated by a few more lines than ages ago when we'd met, but still smooth. Usually, she wore earrings. Not this morning. No watch, no jewelry or makeup. She'd rushed out too quickly to bother.

I felt a nudge at my ankle, heard a wheeze and a snort. Spike grumbled and butted my shin. We'd both adopted him, but he'd adopted her.

"Call off your beast," I said.

Robin laughed and took the coffee. "Thanks, baby." She touched my face. Spike growled louder. She told him, "Don't worry, you're still my handsome."

Setting the cup down, she wrapped both her arms around my neck. Spike produced a poor excuse for a bark, raspy and attenuated by his stubby bulldog larynx.

"Oh, Spikey," she told him, snaring her fingers in my hair.

"If you stop to pet him," I said, "*I'll* start snorting."

"Stop what?"

"This." I kissed her, ran my hands over her back, down to her rear, then up again, grazing her shoulder blades. Starting at the top and kneading the knobs of her spine.

"Oh that's good. I'm a little sore."

"Bad posture," I said. "Not that I'd ever preach."

"No, nothing like that."

We kissed again, more deeply. She relaxed, allowing her body—all 110 pounds of it—to depend upon mine. I felt the warmth of her breath at my ear as I undid the straps of her overalls. The denim fell to her waist but no farther, blocked by the rim of the workbench. I stroked her left arm, luxuriating in the feel of firm muscle under soft skin. Slipping my fingers under her T-shirt, I aimed for the spot that tended to pain her—two spots, really, a pair of knots just above her gluteal cleft. Robin's by no means skeletal; she's a curvy woman, blessed with hips and thighs and breasts and that sheath of body fat that is so wonderfully female. But a small frame meant a back narrow enough for one of my hands to cover both tendernesses simultaneously.

She arched toward me. "Oh . . . you're bad."

"Thought it felt good."

"That's why you're bad. I should be working."

"I should be, too." I took her chin in one hand. Reached down with my other hand and cupped her bottom. No jewelry or makeup, but she had taken the time for perfume, and the fragrance radiated at the juncture of jawline and jugular.

Back to the sore spots.

"Fine, go ahead," she whispered. "Now that you've corrupted me and I'm completely distracted." Her fingers fumbled at my zipper.

"Corruption?" I said. "This is nothing."

I touched her. She moaned. Spike went nuts.

She said, "I feel like an abusive parent." Then she put him outside.

When we finished, the coffee was long cold but we drank it anyway. The red scarf was on the floor and the wood shavings were no longer in a neat pile. I was sitting in an old leather chair, naked, with Robin on my lap. Still breathing hard, still wanting to kiss her. Finally, she pulled away, stood, got dressed, returned to the guitar top. A private-joke smile graced her lips.

"What?"

"We moved around a bit. Just want to make sure we didn't get anything on my masterpiece."

"Like what?"

"Like sweat."

"Maybe that would be a good thing," I said. "Truly organic luthiery."

"Orgasmic luthiery."

"That, too." I got up and stood behind her, smelling her hair. "I love you."

"Love you, too." She laughed. "You are such a *guy*."

"Is that a compliment?"

"Depends on my mood. At this moment, it's a whimsical observation. Every time we make love you tell me you love me."

"That's good, right? A guy who expresses his feelings."

"It's great," she said quickly. "And you're very consistent."

"I tell you other times, don't I?"

"Of course you do, but this is . . ."

"Predictable."

"One hundred percent."

"So," I said, "Professor Castagna has been keeping a record?"

"Don't have to. Not that I'm complaining, sweetie. You can always tell me you love me. I just think it's cute."

"My predictability."

"Better that than instability."

"Well," I said, "I can vary it—say it in another language—how about Hungarian? Should I call Berlitz?"

She pecked my cheek, picked up her chisel.

"Pure guy," she said.

Spike began scratching at the door. I let him in and he raced past me, came to a short stop at Robin's feet, rolled over and presented his abdomen. She kneeled and rubbed him, and his short legs flailed ecstatically.

I said, "Oh you Jezebel. Okay, back to the sawmill."

"No saw today. Just this." Indicating the chisel.

"I meant me."

She looked at me over her shoulder. "Tough day ahead?"

"The usual," I said. "Other people's problems. Which is what I get paid for, right?"

"How'd your meeting with Milo go? Has he learned anything about Dr. Mate?"

"Not so far. He asked me to do some research on Mate, thought I'd try the computer first."

"Shouldn't be hard to produce hits on Mate."

"No doubt," I said. "But finding something valuable in the slag heap's another story. If I dead-end, I'll try the research library, maybe Bio-Med."

"I'll be here all day," she said. "If you don't interrupt me, I'll push my hands too far. How about an early dinner?"

"Sure."

"I mean, baby, don't stay away. I want to hear you say you love me."

Pure guy.

Often, especially after a day when I'd seen more patients than usual, we spent evenings where I did very little talking. Despite all my training, sometimes getting the words out got lost on the highway between Head and Mouth. Sometimes I thought about the nice things I'd tell her, but never followed through.

But when we made love . . . for me, the physical released the emotional and I supposed that put me in some sort of Y-chromosome file box.

There's a common belief that men use love to get sex and women do just the opposite. Like most alleged wisdom about human beings, it's anything but absolute; I've known women who turned thoughtless promiscuity into a fine art and men so bound by affection that the idea of stranger-sex repulsed them to the point of impotence.

I'd never been sure where Richard Doss fell along that continuum. By the time I met him, he hadn't made love to his wife for over three years.

He told me so within minutes of entering the office. As if it was important for me to know of his deprivation. He'd resisted any notion of anyone but his daughter being my patient, yet began by talking about himself. If he was trying to clarify something, I never figured out what it was.

He'd met Joanne Heckler in college, termed the match "ideal," offered the fact that he'd stayed married to her over twenty years as proof. When I met him, she'd been dead for ninety-three days, but he spoke of her as having existed in a very distant past. When he professed to have loved her deeply, I had no reason to doubt him, other than the absence of feeling in his voice, eyes, body posture.

Not that he was incapable of emotion. When I opened the side door that leads to my office, he burst into the house talking on a tiny silver cell phone, continuing to talk in an animated tone after we'd entered the office and I'd sat behind my desk. Wagging an index finger to let me know it would be a minute.

Finally, he said, "Okay, gotta go, Scott. Work the spread, at this point that's the key. If they give us the rate they promised, we're in like Flynn. Otherwise it's a deal-killer. Get them to commit now, not later, Scott. You know the drill."

Eyes flashing, free hand waving.

Enjoying it.

He said, "We'll chat later," clicked off the phone, sat, crossed his legs.

"Negotiations?" I said.

"The usual. Okay, first Joanne." At his mention of his wife's name, his voice went dead.

Physically, he wasn't what I'd expected. My training is supposed to endow me with an open mind, but everyone develops preconceptions, and my mental picture of Richard Doss had been based upon what Judy Manitow had told me and five minutes of phone-sparring.

Aggressive, articulate, dominant. Ex–frat boy, tennis-playing country-club member. Tennis partner of Bob Manitow, who was a physician but about as corporate-looking as you could get. For no good reason, I'd guessed someone who looked like Bob: tall, imposing, a bit beefy, the basic CEO hairstyle: short and side-parted, silver at the temples. A well-cut suit in a somber shade, white or blue shirt, power tie, shiny wing-tips.

Richard Doss was five-five, tops, with a weathered leprechaun face—wide at the brow tapering to an almost womanish point at the chin. A dancer's build, very lean, with square shoulders, a narrow waist. Oversize hands sporting manicured nails coated with clear polish. Palm Springs tan, the kind you rarely saw anymore because of the melanoma scare. The fibrous complexion of one who ignores melanoma warnings.

His hair was black, kinky, and he wore it long enough to evoke another decade. White man's afro. Thin gold chain around his neck. His black silk shirt had flap pockets and buccaneer sleeves and he'd left the top two buttons undone, advertising a hairless chest and extension of the tan. Baggy, tailored gray tweed slacks were held in place by a lizard-skin belt with a silver buckle. Matching loafers, no socks. He carried a smallish black purselike thing in one hand, the silver phone in the other.

I would've pegged him as Joe Hollywood. One of those producer wanna-bes you see hanging out at Sunset Plaza cafés. The type with cheap apartments on month-to-month, poorly maintained leased Corniches, too much leisure time, schemes masquerading as ideas.

Richard Doss had made his way south from Palo Alto and embraced the L.A. image almost to the point of parody.

He said, "My wife was a testament to the failure of modern medicine." The silver phone rang. He jammed it to his ear. "Hi. What? Okay. Good. . . . No, not now. Bye." Click. "Where was I—modern medicine. We saw dozens of doctors. They put her through every test in the book. CAT scans, MRIs, serologic, toxicologic. She had two lumbar punctures. No real reason, I found out later. The neurologist was just 'fishing around.' "

"What were her symptoms?" I said.

"Joint pain, headaches, skin sensitivity, fatigue. It started out as fatigue. She'd always been a ball of energy. Five-two, a hundred and ten pounds. She used to dance, play tennis, powerwalk. The change was gradual—at first I figured a flu, or one of those crazy viruses that's going around. I figured the best thing was stay out of her face, give her time to rest. By the time I realized something serious was going on, she was hard to reach. On another planet." He hooked a finger under the gold chain. "Joanne's parents didn't live long, maybe her constitution . . . She'd always been into the mom thing, that went, too. I suppose *that* was her main symptom. Disengagement. From me, the kids, everything."

"Judy told me she was a microbiologist. What kinds of things did she work on?"

He shook his head. "You're hypothesizing the obvious: she was infected by some pathogen from her lab. Logical but wrong. That was looked into right away, from every angle—some sort of rogue microbe, allergies, hypersensitivity to a chemical. She worked with germs, all right, but they were *plant* germs—vegetable pathogens—molds and funguses that affect food crops. Broccoli, specifically. She had a USDA grant to study broccoli. Do you like broccoli?"

"Sure."

"I don't. As it turns out, there *are* cross-sensitivities between plants and animals, but nothing Joanne worked with fit that category—her equipment, her reagents. She went through every blood test known to medicine." He thumbed black silk cuff. His watch was black-faced with a gold band, so skinny it looked like a tattoo.

"Let's not get distracted," he said. "The precise reason for what happened to Joanne will never be known. Back to the core issue: her disengagement. The first thing to go was entertaining and socializing. She refused to go out with anyone. No more business dinners—too tired, not hungry. Even though all she did in bed was eat. We're members of the Cliffside Country Club and she'd played tennis and a little golf, used the gym. No more. Soon, she was going to bed earlier and rising later. Eventually, she started spending all her time in bed, saying the pain had gotten worse. I told her she might be aching because of inactivity—her muscles were contracting, stiffening up. She didn't answer me. That's when I started taking her to doctors."

He recrossed his legs. "Then there was the weight gain. The only thing she *didn't* withdraw from was food. Cookies, cake, potato chips, anything sweet or greasy." His lips curled, as if he'd tasted something bad. "By the end she weighed two hundred ten pounds. Had more than doubled her weight in less than a year. A hundred and ten extra pounds of pure fat—isn't that incredible, Doctor? It was hard to keep seeing her as the girl I married. She used to be lithe. Athletic. All of a sudden I was married to a stranger—some asexual alien. You're with someone for twenty-five years you just don't stop liking them, but I won't deny it, my feelings for her changed—for all practical purposes she was no longer my wife. I tried to help her with the food. Suggesting maybe she'd be just as satisfied with fruit as with Oreos. But she wouldn't hear of it and she arranged the grocery deliveries when I was at work. I suppose I could've taken drastic measures—gotten her on fen-phen, bolted the refrigerator, but food seemed to be the only thing that kept her going. I felt it was cruel to withdraw it from her."

"I assume every metabolic link was checked out."

"Thyroid, pituitary, adrenal, you name it. I know enough to be an endocrinologist. The weight gain was simply Joanne drowning herself in food. When I made suggestions about cutting back, she responded the same way she did to any opinion I offered. By turning off completely—here, look."

Out of the purse came a pair of plastic-encased snapshots. He made no effort to hand them to me, merely stretched out his arm so I had to get up from my chair to retrieve them.

"Before and after," he said.

The left photo was a color shot of a young couple. Green lawn, big trees, imposing beige buildings. I'd collaborated with a Stanford professor on a research project years ago, recognized the campus.

"I was a senior, she was a sophomore," said Doss. "That was taken right after we got engaged."

For many students, the seventies had meant long coifs, facial hair, torn jeans and sandals. Counterculture giving way to Brooks Brothers only when the realities of making a living sank in.

It was as if Richard Doss had reversed the process. His college 'do had been a dense black crew cut. In the picture he wore a white shirt, pressed gray slacks, horn-rimmed glasses. And here were the shiny black wing-tips. Study-pallor on the elfin face, no tan.

Youthful progenitor of the corporate type I'd expected him to be.

Distracted expression. No celebration of the engagement that I could detect.

The girl under his arm was smiling. Joanne Heckler, petite as described, had been pretty in a well-scrubbed way. Fair-skinned and narrow-faced, she wore her brown hair long and straight, topped by a white band. Glasses for her, too. Smaller than Richard's, and gold-framed. A diamond glinted on her ring finger. Her sleeveless dress was bright blue, modest for that era.

Another elf. Marriage of the leprechauns.

They say couples who live together long enough start to look like each other. Richard and Joanne had begun that way but diverged.

I turned to the second photo, a washed-out Polaroid. A subject who resembled no one.

Long-view of a king-size bed, shot from the foot. Rumpled gold comforter strewn across a tapestry-covered bed bench. High mound of beige pillows propped against the headboard. In their midst, a head floated.

White face. Round. So porcine and bloated the features were compressed to a smear. Bladder-cheeks. Eyes buried in folds. Just a hint of brown hair tied back tight from a pasty forehead. Pucker-mouth devoid of expression.

Below the head, beige sheets rose like a bell-curved, tented bulk. To the right was an elegant carved nightstand in some kind of dark, glossy wood, with gold pulls. Behind the headboard was peach wallpaper printed with teal flowers. A length of gilded frame and linen mat hinted at artwork cropped out of the photo.

For one shocking moment, I wondered if Richard Doss had a post-mortem shot. But no, the eyes were open . . . something in them . . . despair? No, worse. A living death.

"Eric took it," said Doss. "My son. He wanted a record."

"Of his mom?" I said. Hoarse, I cleared my throat.

"Of what had happened to his mom. Frankly put, it pissed him off."

"He was angry at her?"

"No," he said, as if I were an idiot. "At the situation. That's how my son deals with his anger."

"By documenting?"

"By organizing. Putting things in their place. Personally, I think it's a great way to handle stress. Lets you wade through the emotional garbage, analyze the factual content of events, get in touch with how you feel, then move on. Because what choice is there? Wallow in other people's misery? Allow yourself to be destroyed?"

He pointed a finger at me, as if I'd accused him of something.

"If that sounds callous," he said, "so be it, Doctor. You haven't lived in my house, never went through what I did. Joanne took over a year to leave us. We had time to figure things out. Eric's a brilliant boy—the smartest person I've ever met. Even so, it affected him. He was in his second semester at Stanford, came home to be with Joanne. He devoted himself to her, so if taking that picture seems callous, bear that in mind. And it's not as if his mother minded. She just lay there—that picture captures exactly what she was like at the end. How she ever mobilized the energy to contact the sonofabitch who killed her I'll never know."

"Dr. Mate."

He ignored me, fingered the silver phone. Finally our eyes met. I smiled, trying to let him know I wasn't judging. His lids were slightly lowered. Beneath them, dark eyes shone like nuggets of coal.

"I'll take those back." He leaned forward, holding out his hand for the pictures. Again, I had to stand to return them.

"How did Stacy cope?" I said.

He took his time zipping open the purse and placing the snapshots within. Crossing his legs yet again. Massaging the phone, as if hoping a call would rescue him from having to answer.

"Stacy," he said, "is another story."

6

I booted up the computer. Eldon Mate's name pulled up over a hundred sites.

Most of the references were reprints of newspaper columns covering Mate's career as a one-way travel agent. Pros, cons, no shortage of strong opinions from experts on both sides. Everyone responding on an intellectual level. Nothing psychopathic, none of the cold cruelty that had flavored the murder.

A "Dr. Death Home Page" featured a flattering photo of Mate, recaps of his acquittals and a brief biography. Mate had been born in San Diego sixty-three years ago, received a degree in chemistry from San Diego State and worked as a chemist for an oil company before entering medical school in Guadalajara, Mexico, at the age of forty. He'd served an internship at a hospital in Oakland, gotten licensed as a general practitioner at forty-six.

No specialty training. The only jobs the news pieces had mentioned were civil service positions at health departments all over the

Southwest, where Mate had overseen immunization programs and pushed paper. No indication he'd ever treated a patient.

Beginning a new career as a doctor in middle age but avoiding contact with the living. Had he been drawn to medicine in order to get closer to death?

The name and phone number at the bottom of the page was Attorney Roy Haiselden's. He'd listed no e-mail address.

Next came several euthanasia stories:

The first few covered the case of Roger Damon Sharveneau, a respiratory therapist at a hospital in Rochester, New York, who'd confessed eighteen months earlier to snuffing out three dozen intensive-care patients by injecting potassium chloride into their I.V. lines—wanting to "ease their journey." Sharveneau's lawyer claimed his client was insane, had him examined by a psychiatrist who diagnosed borderline personality and prescribed the antidepressant imipramine. A few days later, Sharveneau recanted. Without his confession, the only evidence against him was proximity to the ICU every night a questionable death had occurred. The same applied to three other techs, so the police released Sharveneau, terming the case "still under investigation." Sharveneau filed for disability benefits, granted an interview to a local newspaper and claimed he'd been under the influence of a shadowy figure named Dr. Burke, whom no one had ever seen. Soon after, he overdosed fatally on imipramine.

The case prompted an investigation of other respiratory techs living in the Rochester area. Several with criminal backgrounds were found working at hospitals and convalescent homes around the state. The health commissioner vowed to institute tighter controls.

I plugged Sharveneau's name into the system, found only one follow-up article that cited lack of progress on the original investigation and doubts as to whether the thirty-six deaths had been unnatural.

The next link was a decade-old case: four nurses in Vienna had killed as many as three hundred people using overdoses of morphine and insulin. Arrest, conviction, sentences ranging from fifteen years to life. Eldon Mate was quoted as suggesting the killers might have been acting out of compassion.

A similar case from Chicago: two years later, a pair of nurses' aides who'd smothered elderly terminal patients to death as part of a lesbian romance. Plea bargain for the one who talked, life without parole for the other. Once again, Mate had offered a contrarian opinion.

Onward. A Cleveland piece dated only two months earlier. Kevin Arthur Haupt, an emergency medical tech working the night shift on a city ambulance, had decided to shortcut the treatment of twelve drunks he'd picked up on heart-attack calls by clamping his hand over their noses and mouths during transport to the hospital. Discovery came when one of the intended victims turned out to be healthier than expected, awoke to find himself being smothered and fought back. Arrest, multiple murder charge, guilty plea, thirty-year sentence. Mate wondered in print if spending money to resuscitate habitual alcoholics was a wise use of tax dollars.

An old wire-service piece about the Netherlands, where assisted suicide was no longer prosecuted, claimed that doctor-initiated killings had grown to 2 percent of all recorded Dutch deaths, with 25 percent of physicians admitting they'd euthanized patients deemed unfit to live, without the patients' consent.

Years ago, while working Western Pediatrics Medical Center, I'd served on something called the Ad Hoc Life Support Committee—six physicians and myself, drafted by the hospital board to come up with guidelines for ending the treatment of children in final-stage illness. We'd been a fractious group, producing debate and very little else. But each of us knew that scarcely a month went by when a slightly-larger-than-usual dose of morphine didn't find its way into the mesh of tubes attached to a tiny arm. Kids suffering from bone or brain cancer, atrophied livers, ravaged lungs, who just happened to "stop breathing," once their parents had said good-bye.

Some caring soul ending the pain of a child who would've died anyway, sparing the family the agony of a protracted deathwatch.

The same motivation claimed by Eldon H. Mate.

Why did it feel different to me from Mate's gloating use of the Humanitron?

Because I believed the doctors and nurses on cancer wards had been acting out of compassion, but I suspected Mate's motivations?

Because Mate came across obnoxious and publicity-seeking?

Was that the worst type of hypocrisy on my part, accepting covert god-play from those I greeted in the hall while allowing myself to be repelled by Mate's in-your-face approach to death? So what if the screeching little man with the homemade killing machine wouldn't have won any charm contests. Did the *psyche* of the travel agent matter when the final *destination* was always the same?

My father had died quietly, fading away from cirrhosis and kidney failure and general breakdown of his body after a lifetime of bad habits. Muscles reabsorbing, skin bagging as he devolved into a wizened, yellowed gnome I hardly recognized.

As the poisons in his system accumulated, it took only a few weeks for Harry Delaware to sink from lethargy to torpor to coma. If he'd gone out screaming in agony, would I now harbor any reservations about the Humanitron?

And what about people like Joanne Doss, suffering but undiagnosed?

If you accepted death as a civil rights issue, did a medical label matter? Whose life *was* it, anyway?

Religion supplied answers, but when you took God out of the equation, things got complicated. That was as good a reason as any for God, I supposed. I wished I'd been blessed with a greater capacity for faith and obedience. What would happen if one day I found myself being devoured by cancer, or deadened by paralysis?

Sitting there, hand poised to strike the ENTER key, I found that my thoughts kept flying back to my father's last days. Strange—he rarely came to mind.

Then I pictured Dad as a healthy man. Big bald head, creased bull neck, sandpaper hands from all those years turning wood on the lathe. Alcohol breath and tobacco laughter. One-handed push-ups, the too-hard slap on the back. He'd been well into his fifties by the time I could hold my own against him in the arm wrestles he demanded as a greeting ritual during my increasingly rare trips back to Missouri.

I found myself edging forward on the chair. Positioning myself for combat, just as I'd done as Dad's forearm and mine pressed against each other, hot and sticky. Elbows slipping on the Formica of the kitchen table as we purpled and strained, muscles quivering with tetany. Mom leaving the room, looking pained.

By the time Dad hit fifty-five, the pattern was set: mostly I'd win, occasionally we'd tie. He'd laugh at first.

Alexander-er, when I was young I could climb walls!

Then he'd light up a Chesterfield, frown and mutter, leave the room. My visits thinned to once a year. The ten days I spent sitting silently holding my mother's hand as he died was my longest stay since leaving home for college.

I shuttered the memories, tried to relax, punched a key. The computer—perfect, silent companion that it was—obliged by flashing a new image.

A site posted by a Washington, D.C.–based handicapped-rights group named Still Alive. A position statement: all human life was precious, no one should judge anyone else's quality of life. Then a section on Mate—to this group, Hitler incarnate. Archival photo of Still Alive members picketing a motel where Mate had left a traveler. Men and women in wheelchairs, lofting banners. Mate's reaction to the protest: "You're a bunch of whiners who should examine your own selfish motivations."

Quotes from Mate and Roy Haiselden followed:

"The storm troopers came for me, but I wouldn't play passive Jew" (Mate, 1991).

"Darwin would have loved to meet [District Attorney] Clarkson. The idiot's living proof of the missing link between pond slime and mammalian organisms" (Haiselden, 1993).

"A needle in a vein is a hell of a lot more humane than a nuclear bomb, but you don't hear much outrage from the morality mongoloids about atomic testing, do you?" (Mate, 1995).

"Any pioneer, anyone with a vision, inevitably suffers. Jesus, Buddha, Copernicus, the Wright brothers. Hell, the guy who invented stickum on envelopes probably got abused by the idiots who manufactured sealing wax" (Mate, 1995).

"Sure, I'd go on *The Tonight Show,* but it ain't gonna happen, folks! Too many stupid rules imposed by the network. Hell, I'd help someone *travel* on *The Tonight Show* if the fools who made the rules would let me. I'd do it live—so to speak. It would be their highest-rated show, I can promise you that. They could play it during sweeps week. I'd play some music in the background—something classical. Use some poor soul with a totally compromised nervous system—maybe an advanced muscular dystrophy case—limbs out of control, tongue flapping, copious salivation, no bladder or bowel control—let them leak all over the soundstage, show the world how pretty decay and disease are. If I could do that, you'd see all that sanctimonious drivel about the nobility of life fade away pronto. I could pull off the whole thing in minutes, safe, clean, silent. Let the camera focus on the traveler's face, show how peaceful they were once the thiopental kicked in. Teach the world that the true nature of compassion isn't some priest or rabbi claiming to be God's holy messenger or some government mongoloid lackey who couldn't pass a basic biology course trying to tell me what's life and what isn't. 'Cause it's not that complex, amigos: when the brain ain't workin', you ain't livin.' *The Tonight Show* . . . yeah, that would be educational. If they let me set it up the right way, sure, I'd do it" (Mate, 1997, in response to a press question about why he liked publicity).

"Dr. Mate should get the Nobel Prize. Double payment. For medicine *and* peace. I wouldn't mind a piece of that, myself. Being his lawyer, I deserve it" (Haiselden, 1998).

Other assorted oddities, ranked lower for relevance:

A three-year-old Denver news item about a Colorado "outsider" artist with the improbable name of Zero Tollrance who'd created a series of paintings inspired by Mate and his machine. Using an abandoned building in a run-down section of Denver, Tollrance, previously unknown, had exhibited thirty canvases. A freelance writer had covered the show for *The Denver Post,* citing "several portraits of the controversial 'death doctor' in a wide range of familiar poses: Gilbert Stuart's George Washington, Thomas Gainsborough's Blue Boy, Vincent van Gogh's bandaged-ear self-portrait, Andy Warhol's Marilyn Monroe. Non-Mate works included collages of coffins, cadavers, skulls and maggot-infested meat. But perhaps the most ambitious of Tollrance's productions is a faithfully rendered re-creation of Rembrandt's *Anatomy Lesson,* a graphic portrayal of human dissection, with Dr. Mate serving a dual role, as scalpel-wielding lecturer as well as flayed cadaver."

When asked how many paintings had sold, Tollrance "walked away without comment."

Mate as cutter and victim. Be interesting to talk to Mr. Tollrance. Save. Print.

Two citations from a health-issues academic bulletin board posted by Harvard University: a geriatric study found that while 59.3 percent of the relatives of elderly patients favored legalizing physician-assisted suicide, only 39.9 percent of the old people agreed. And a study done at a cancer treatment center found that two thirds of the American public endorsed assisted death but 88 percent of cancer patients suffering from constant pain had no interest in exploring the topic and felt that a doctor's bringing it up would erode their trust.

In a feminist resource site I found an article in a journal called *S(Hero)* entitled "Mercy or Misogyny: Does Dr. Mate Have a Problem with Women?" The author wondered why 80 percent of Mate's "travelers" had been female. Mate, she claimed, had never been known to have a relationship with a woman and had refused to answer questions about his personal life. Freudian speculation followed.

Milo hadn't mentioned any family. I made a note to follow up on that.

The final item: four years ago, in San Francisco, a group calling itself the Secular Humanist Infantry had granted Mate its highest award, the Heretic. Prior to the ceremony, a syringe Mate had used on a recent "travel venture" had been auctioned off for two hundred dollars, only to be confiscated immediately by an undercover police officer citing violation of state health regulations. Commotion and protest as the cop dropped the needle into an evidence bag and exited. During his acceptance speech, Mate donated his windbreaker as a consolation prize and termed the officer a "mental gnat with all the morals of a rotavirus."

The name of the winning bidder caught my eye.

Alice Zoghbie. Treasurer of the Secular Humanist Infantry, now president of the Socrates Club. The same woman who'd leased the death van and left that day for Amsterdam.

I ran a search on the club, found the home page, topped by a logo of the Greek philosopher's sculpted head surrounded by a wreath that

I assumed was hemlock. As Milo'd said, headquarters on Glenmont Circle in Glendale, California.

The Socrates mission statement emphasized the "personal owner-ship of life, unfettered by the outmoded and barbaric conventions foisted upon society by organized religion." Signed, Alice Zoghbie, MPA. A hundred-dollar fee entitled the fortunate to notification of events and all other benefits of membership. AMEX, VISA, MC, and DISC accepted.

Zoghbie's master's in public administration didn't tell me much about her professional background. Searching her name produced a long article in *The San Jose Mercury News* that filled in the blanks.

Entitled "Right-to-Die Group's Leader's Comments Cause Con-troversy," the piece described Zoghbie as

> fiftyish, pencil-thin and tall. The former hospital personnel director is now engaged full-time running the Socrates Club, an organization devoted to legalizing assisted suicide. Until recently, members have maintained a low profile, concen-trating upon filing friend-of-court briefs in right-to-die cases. However, recent remarks by Zoghbie at last Sunday's brunch at the Western Sun Inn here in San Jose have cast the club into the limelight and raised questions about its true goals.
>
> During the meeting, attended by an estimated fifty peo-ple, Zoghbie delivered a speech calling for the "humane dis-patch of patients with Alzheimer's disease and other types of 'thought impairment,' " as well as disabled children and oth-ers who are legally incapable of making "the decision they'd clearly form if they were in their right minds."
>
> "I worked at a hospital for twenty years," the tan, white-haired woman said, "and I witnessed firsthand the abuses that took place in the name of treatment. Real compassion isn't creating vegetables. Real compassion is scientists putting their heads together to create a measurement scale that would quantify suffering. Those who score above a pre-determined criterion could then be helped in a timely man-ner even if they lacked the capacity to liberate themselves."
>
> Reaction to Zoghbie's proposal by local religious leaders was swift and negative. Catholic Bishop Armand Rodriguez termed the plan "a call to genocide," and Dr. Archie Van

Sandt of the Mount Zion Baptist Church accused Zoghbie of
being "an instrument of cancerous secularism." Rabbi Eu-
gene Brandner of Temple Emanu-El said that Zoghbie's
ideas were "certainly not in line with Jewish thought at any
point along the spectrum."

An unattributed statement by the Socrates Club issued
two days later attempted to qualify Zoghbie's remarks,
terming them "an impetus to discussion rather than a policy
statement."

Dr. J. Randolph Smith, director of the Western Medical
Association's Committee on Medical Ethics, viewed the dis-
avowal with some skepticism. "A simple reading of the tran-
script shows this was a perfectly clear expression of
philosophy and intent. The slippery slope yawns before us,
and groups such as the Socrates Club seem intent on shov-
ing us down into the abyss of amorality. Given further acceptance of views such as Ms. Zoghbie's, it's only a matter of
time before the legalization of murder of those who say they
want to die gives way to the murder of those who have never
asked to die, as is now the case in the Netherlands."

I logged off, called Milo at the station. A young man answered his
phone, asked me who I was with some suspicion and put me on hold.

A few seconds later, Milo said, "Hi."

"New secretary?"

"Detective Stephen Korn. One of my little helpers. What's up?"

"Got some stuff for you, but nothing profound." Got a resolved
ethical issue, too, but I'll save that for later.

"What kind of stuff?" he said.

"Mostly biography and the expected controversy, but Alice Zoghbie's name came up—"

"Alice Zoghbie just called me," he said. "Back in L.A. and willing to
talk."

"Thought she wasn't due for two days."

"She cut her trip short. Distraught about Mate."

"Delayed grief reaction?" I said. "Mate's been dead for a week."

"She claims she didn't hear about it till yesterday. Was up in Nepal
somewhere—climbing mountains, the Amsterdam thing was the tail
end of her trip, big confab of death freaks from all over the world. Not